DOMESTIC

JURANAMO JONES

AUTHORS INSIGHT

When I first started writing this book, I looked at it as just a part two, of *The Sweetest Joy* series. The more I continued to write and rough draft this fictional story, the more interested I became in highlighting the overlooked everyday problems of domestic violence. So, I did more research and realized how much domestic violence affects our everyday lives and future. Even if not directly, it's indirectly.

In the U.S. alone, the population is 330,228,635 as of February 5, 2020.

Sources on Wikipedia reported, that there are between 960,000 and 3,000,000 incidents of domestic violence reported each year while many more go unreported. They also reported, that it is an estimate of more than ten million people that experience domestic violence in the U.S. each year. There are only nine states in the U.S. with more than ten million people living there.

The National Coalition Against Domestic Violence (NCADV) reported, that there is an incident of physical abuse in the U.S. every 20 minutes. Intimate partner violence accounts for 15% of all violent crimes.

Many result in permanent mental and physical injuries, and some become fatal. Not only are lives lost but money is too, which can increase the chances of other crimes just to provide for ones' family or self.

The NCADV reported, that victims of intimate partner violence lose a total of 8.0 million days of work each year. 21% to 60% of intimate partner violence victims/participants lose their employment because of the acts.

Domestic Violence runs deeper than just physical altercations. Verbal altercations, which cause mental abuse also, play a major part in it all. Mental abuse often turns into physical abuse because of emotion. To me, mental and physical abuse run hand in hand. One is no greater than the other, even if law enforcement beg to differ.

No, I do not expect domestic violence to just stop throughout the world, but I do expect us as adults to become more responsible and practice prevention. To work on ourselves as well as our emotions, to protect ourselves as well as our future.

And yes, this is the second time you've seen me use the word, "**Future**." When I refer to future, I'm not only talking about our personal tomorrows, but I'm more so referring to the real future—the children of tomorrow. We must adjust our outlooks on life for the sake of our children's future. We must reflect on what we have done yesterday to understand why our todays behave in their manner tomorrow.

The NCADV reported that 1 in 15 children are exposed to intimate partner violence each year. 90% of the children are eyewitnesses to the violence.

Victims as well as witnesses of physical violence tend to suffer from mental health disorders.

PTSD, anxiety, suicidal behavior, homicidal behavior, as well as being anti-social, are just a few signs of physical violence victims/witnesses.

Victims/witnesses, are also more likely to embrace addictions to alcohol, tobacco and drugs, which are supposed to help easily deal with PTSD, anxiety, and other internal mental disorders.

At the end of the day, our actions are less about our current emotions, and more about our future. Though, some of us adults can simply adjust to the trials of life, our unconscious, selfish thought patterns don't stop and take a second to realize who the real losers are throughout it all. And those are our children.

So, if you really love and respect, your future, your children, as much as you claim you do, how about you first do what is best for your children, and not just yourself and "practice prevention".

Remember, emotion is only a feeling. A feeling that can be dissatisfying in one moment, and satisfying the next. It's a temporary feeling, which can only make you wiser and stronger, if you shall master the art of self-control. Your future will be thankful you did.

Enjoy the story!

    -Juranamo Jones

PRELUDE

It's been 4 years now and I've decided that now is the perfect time to reach out to you for closure. I've been wanting to write you for years, but couldn't figure out where to start. I just want to let you know that I am sorry for everything that has happened and wish it all could've been different. I've realized, I lost a lot but you have lost more. I can admit that I was bitter and upset for the first couple of years, but after a few counseling sessions, I've overcame what I cannot control. I'm now older and 7 months pregnant, expecting my first child. It's supposed to be a boy. I would be honored if you named him. Well, I pray on your appeals success, and hope you are released soon. May God bless you and stay strong. I will be expecting a letter back soon.

Sincerely,

Sarah

My name is Derrick Jones. I'm currently incarcerated in a Level seven, federal penitentiary, in Pennsylvania, called *U.S.P Canaan.* I've been sentenced to 396 months, in prison, by a Superior Court, judge, out of Washington, DC, for 1st degree murder, 2nd degree murder, attempted robbery, and possession of a firearm in the use of a crime of violence. I've been in prison for 50 months now, and my direct appeal has been pending for about two years. I pray, to hear some good news soon, because this is not the life I had imagined for myself. Everything in here is geographical and racist. This is my first time ever being arrested, and I got hit with 33 years, of prison time. Some luck huh? I can admit, though I grew up in the hood, I was far from the hood type. I was a Class A, truck driver, working for *Coca-Cola*, making no less than $70K, a year. Also, I was a Certified Master Barber too. A skill I didn't utilize much until I came to prison. Now, I'm in prison studying books on stock investing, and non-profit organizations. I mean, I never sold drugs a day in my life, let alone shot a gun until....

I know, by now, you're wondering how my perfect little life made a sudden twist towards doom. Yeah, I would be too. Where do I start? From the beginning, always makes sense.

CHAPTER I

I was born on October 31, 1991, in *Howard University Hospital Center,* in Northwest, DC, to my mom Karen Jones, and my pops Marvin Jones. My first name is Marvin, but I've been going by my middle name, Derrick, my entire life. So, that's what I introduce myself as, Derrick Jones. I was a Jr., to a street hustler everybody used to call Marty. My dad was murdered when I was just two years young. A guy tried to rob my pops, and he refused to give up his wealth without a fight, which resulted in a scuffle over the gun. In the heat of the battle, the robber pulled the trigger and became a killer. A lot of the older street dudes that knew my pops, always spoke highly of him. They always put emphasis on "he was a man of respect," who took pride in providing for, as well as protecting, his family.

I wish I would've been provided the chance to know him better, but I guess God had other plans. We lived in Northeast, DC, around a neighborhood called, *Mayfair Mansions.* Mayfair, is a big neighborhood. Too big of a neighborhood, for little ol' me. A lot of people I come across can't even believe that I lived around there due to the high crime rate. Crime and I, do not match. I remember, one day I tried to steal an ice cream sandwich from the local corner store and got caught. I put it in my pocket and froze up, as soon as I got to the front door. The store owner, Mr. Emanuel, walked over to me, dug in my pockets, and took the ice cream sandwich out of it.

"Next time you ask. This is not for you." Emanuel demanded, before handing me the ice cream sandwich. "Now go" is what he said, before I ran out of the store with the ice cream sandwich freezing my fingers. He never told my mom on me, and I respected him to this day for that.

My mom was a heavy crack smoker. My sister said, my mom got addicted after my pops death. My mom, used to let one of the local hustlers named Trukhead, hustle out of her apartment, since he helped pay the bills. Then that's when it all happened....

Trukhead, was a real cool, laid back dude. He always looked out for my sister Kendra, and I. He sometimes brought us school clothes and supplies until he got arrested for murder in 1996. My mom was disturbed after Trukhead's arrest, because she no longer had a direct and consistent source to support her habit. Kendra and my mother, used to argue and fight a lot, due to my mom's temper tantrums. Mom not having her hit whenever she wanted it, made her into a very unlikeable person. Kendra, took good care of me, and protected me like I was her son. Even from my own mother. Kendra, was eight years my senior. Kendra, started working at *Deane Avenue Cleaners*, on Nannie Helen Burroughs in Northeast, when she was 14. The owner of the cleaners knew about our situation, and gave my sister a part-time job. Though, Kendra, was too young to work anywhere without a work permit, the owner, Ms. Shaw, still employed her, and kept it all under the table by paying Kendra, in cash. Kendra, also did hairstyling on the side, to make sure she and I were taken care of. It was the summer of 2000, when I was only 8 years old. My mom was beaten to death, by her boyfriend, Jeff, who was also a heavy crack smoker.

The witnesses, who were inside of the crack house at the time of the beating, claimed that my mom stole Jeff's last piece of crack when he was sleep and smoked it all. It was rumored, that this wasn't her first time doing it, and it wasn't his first time beating her ass. But it definitely was the last time either of the two would ever see each other. Jeff, was sentenced to 13 years in prison.

Things got really rough for us. Our next door neighbor, Ms. Jackie, took temporary custody of us. Shortly after my moms' death, Kendra, dropped out of high school during her senior year, to work full-time at *McDonald's*. She also found a second job at night, working custodial maintenance at a *Red Roof Inn hotel,* in Maryland. Kendra was dedicated to making our lives comfortable. In the winter of 2002, when I was 11 years young, Kendra and I, moved out of Ms. Jackie's apartment, into a one bedroom apartment on Gault Place, in Northeast. Not too far from our old neighborhood, Mayfair. It was a small six unit apartment building, across the street from *Minnesota Avenue,* subway station. Gault Place, was a really short and compact street, loaded with street hustlers. Though, it was obvious that everybody was breaking law, the respect level for my sister and I was great. A few guys tried to make passes on my sister, but Kendra, didn't give them the time of day. I mean, how could you not try your hand? Kendra, was a very beautiful, petite redbone, who had all of her own hair. Her hair stretched all the way down to the small of her lower back. Kendra, stood about 5'7", and was independent. Though, I honestly believe she was attracted to white men since she had a crush on Zach, from *Saved By The Bell*, she did later give a few hood dudes, a very short term chance. Kendra, used to have posters of body models posted on her bedroom wall, and all of them were white men. Kendra, had only one female friend, Kathy, who was a white girl. Her only real relationship was with this mulatto dude named Mike, from

Virginia. Throughout time, Kendra, grew apart from him. She said, he was a hood reject. He wanted to be looked at as a street dude so bad. Kendra said, "I don't need a hustler, I need a man." I then, respected her more, for her decisions. She knew at a young age exactly what she wanted out of life. Kendra, was not perfect, but she was working on herself to be the perfect her. Sometimes, she and I used to bump heads over her views of black men. She would say things like, "white men are a lot more humble and passive than black men." Very stereotypical, but she was a strong believer. When I used to be out and about with her, guys used to say things like, "You mean as hell" or "I'm not your enemy baby girl." For a second, I was starting to think my sister hated men, but as I grew older, I began to understand Kendra more and more.

FLASHBACK

April 1990

"Stop it, Sal, please just stop it!" I heard my mom frantically pleading, with her deep Italian accent, as I paced through the house trying to pinpoint what the loud noises were I heard almost every night since I had been born.

A thump here, a bang there. My mom begging and pleading for help, or my dad swearing to kill. The closer to the noise I got, the more scared I became. I felt like I was in one of those scary movies my dad forced me to watch before bedtime, when the background music became louder as you got closer to the killer. My dad claimed, that me watching scary movies before bed would help me to never be afraid of anything. And me, as a 12 year old kid, believed any and everything he told me. He had me watching scary movies before bedtime, since I was about six years of age. And honestly, I think he was right. I wasn't even ticklish.

> "Go lay your scrawny ass down before I make ya' next, ya hear!" My dad demanded me, with spit sprinkling from his mouth, as he angrily yelled at me, tightly clutching a black leather belt that I was oh so familiar with.

I looked and saw my mom, curled up on her bed, face full of tears and shaking out of fear, as my dad stood over top of her like the big bad wolf, who had just hunted down his prey. I ran as fast as I could back to my bed, and pretended as if I was already asleep, as I prayed, that I wasn't next.

CHAPTER II

<u>January 2004</u>

"I'ma have to put you in boxing or martial arts classes soon so you can learn how to defend yourself." Kendra said, when my high yellow ass came home from school with another black eye.

I went to *Friendship Public Charter School*, on Minnesota Avenue, which was just barely a five minute walk from our apartment. It was my first year there, and I was glad that it was about over.

So far, seventh grade, was the worst year of school for me. And to top it off, I might be spending my entire summer fighting, or learning how to at the least. I was a straight "A" student, with no more than zero friends. My sister Kendra, kept me fresh and clean, but not up to date. I never in my life owned a pair of *Air Jordan* sneakers, and had only one pair of *NIKE.* I owned about three pair of sneakers, but nothing like the ones all of the other kids had so, I stood out like a sore thumb. People looked at me as "different".

April 2004

For the past three months, Kendra, has been tied up with her new boyfriend, Ralph, and not spending much time with me as she usually does. And from the look of things, she hasn't been spending much time with Kathy, either. Kathy, was always calling, or popping up at our apartment, looking for Kendra, who was highly successful at not wanting to be found. Kathy, played the cat and mouse game with Kendra, so much, a point she just got fed up and gave up.

"Tell her see me when she sees me" was the last thing Kathy, said on the phone to me, about a month ago.

And that was the last time I ever heard anything from, or about Kathy. She just disappeared. Ralph, to my surprise, was actually a black man. A really conservative type of guy, who was big on politics and computers. Kendra said, that he went to high school at *Dematha*, which is a Catholic private school for boys, and is now a junior at *Georgetown University*. A real clean-cut, well-mannered type of guy. I'm really happy for my sister, though, I miss our time spent together. Now, all I have to do is find myself a girlfriend, which seems so taboo. I mean, I'm not the cutest, but I was a long distance from ugly. I was just scrawny looking, and non-athletic. At this time, lightskin was in style, just not me.

"Derrick! Run down the street and grab a loaf of bread and a gallon of milk real quick, while I finish this meal." Kendra demanded, before handing me a five dollar bill. "And make sure it's two percent this time and not whole milk, please!" Kendra specified, as I arose from the couch, snatching the five bucks from her hand, and dragged my feet towards the front door. "And don't be snatching nothing from me little boy!" Kendra yelled.

"Yeah, yeah, yeah, whatever." I mumbled, as I walked out the door, allowing it to slam shut behind me.

I was a little annoyed, because I hated being interrupted while watching, *Power Rangers*. That was my favorite TV show. I walked into *R&M Grocery Deli* corner store, which was Asian owned, bought the bread and milk, and then sped out of the store with the intention of catching what's left of today's episode. As soon as I walked out to the front of the store, here comes Frankie, Mike, and Julio. Frankie, is the guy who blacked my eye. Mike and Julio, were his best friends, but I looked at them more so as his yes men. Mike and Julio, did whatever Frankie demanded.

"Yep lemme get dat." Frankie demanded, as he attempted to reach for my bag of groceries, which made me automatically snatch away and secure the bag.

Frankie, immediately made an angry, but surprised, looking facial expression. Honestly, I was surprised at myself, but I was willing to take a beat down by Frankie, and his crew, before I walked back into my house empty handed.

"Oh yeah! So you bucking huh?" Frankie spat, before following up his words with a punch to my face.

I curled up, to block my face and body from most of the blows that the trio delivered.

"Get the fuck off him!" I heard a deep voice demand, before I looked up and saw an older guy grab Frankie by the back of his neck with one hand, and smacking him in the face with the other.

Mike and Julio, immediately, stopped hitting me and swiftly backpedaled, to avoid being hit by the older guy.

"Get your lil' bitch ass outta here before I fuck you over!" The older guy spat, as he punted Frankie in the butt.

"You aight lil' homie?" The older guy asked as I stood up, nodding my head up and down. "You live over there right?" He asked, pointing toward my building.

"Yeah, I do." I replied nervously.

"Aight come on. Grab your shit." He said, before escorting me to my apartment.

When I walked into the apartment, Kendra's eyes grew wide in surprise.

"What in the hell happened to you that quick!?" Kendra asked, from the kitchen area.

"Some lil' young niggaz jumped him, and tried to rob him, but he ain't give it up." The older guy said, from the doorway.

"And you are?" Kendra, sarcastically asked, the older guy.

"I'm Chris. I live right up the street. I was just helping lil' man out." The older guy replied.

"Oh okay Chris, nice to meet you. You can leave now." Kendra snapped, sarcastically.

"Kendra!" I spat. "He helped me out!"

"Okay cool. And I said thank you too. Now he can take care!" Kendra, spat back at me with a harsh stare.

"It's cool lil' man. I'll see you around soldier. Just let me know if you ever need anything. I'm out'chere." Chris made it clear to me. "Aight Kendra, take care." Chris spat sarcastically, before exhaling a giggle and closing the front door.

"I gotta get you in those classes ASAP!" Kendra said, as she took the groceries from out of my hand. "Go clean yourself up so you can get ready to eat." Kendra said, before I walked into the bathroom.

"And we gotta get you into anger management classes." I mumbled to myself.

"I heard that!" Kendra yelled, from the kitchen.

FLASHBACK

August 1990

"I'm sick and tired of this shit, Sal!" were the last words I heard my mom yell right before….

POW! POW! POW!

After a brief moment of silence, I heard a loud cry then, **POW!** I nervously, sat on the edge of my bed, anticipating, hearing another gunshot, or my mom and dads' voices, yelling at each other as usual. After about three or four minutes of hearing nothing but complete silence, I became curious. That's when I finally decided to feed my curiosity and be nosey. I nervously crept through our home towards my parents' room, whose room door was ajar enough to see inside the room, but not wide enough to see who or what was inside of the room. So, I slowly pushed open the door to get a better view. At that moment, I was then cursed with seeing a sight that would haunt me my entire life. My dad, laid out on his bed in a pool of blood, with his hands pressing down on his chest, as if he was trying to maintain the bleeding. His eyes were open wide, and as big as a golf ball. You could see the fear in them, as if the reality of dying was his worst nightmare, as he choked on a mouth full of blood, while trying to catch his breathing. I then, saw my mom. My mother, was lying to the left of the bed, stretched out on the floor, with a black gun rested beside her right forearm, as if it fell out of her palm. Blood was constantly gushing from her skull, after she delivered herself a fatal shot to the right side of her skull…. Suicide!

CHAPTER III

Things in my life changed tremendously after meeting Chris. He was like the big brother I never had. He would sometimes walk me to and from school, and kept me dressed in the latest gear. I even finally got myself a pair of Jordans. Females, in school was finally looking my way. My confidence was sitting sky high. So high, I even started trying to play sports. I sucked, so you know that didn't last too long. Frankie & Co. never disrespected me again. Actually, for a while, Frankie, never even looked my way, until the last week of school. That's when he attempted to befriend me, by inviting me to his "Summer Break Party". I told him, "I'll see if I can come", but later decided not to show face. I was cool and comfortable with the way things were… Hanging with Chris.

Kendra, on the other hand, was acting a lot different than usual. She would come home and go straight to bed, plus, she wore dark shades a little too often. Even around the house. Her vibe was troubling and out of the ordinary, to a point that I didn't even know how to approach her. Even Chris, noticed her transition. He told me, that Kendra, would never even acknowledge him when he would see her coming in the building or walking down the street. He also said, he once walked up and saw Kendra and her boyfriend arguing in his car, out front of our building, right before Kendra, angrily stormed out of her boyfriend's car, slamming the passenger door, before rushing into our apartment building. Little did Kendra know, Chris, really liked and respected her as much as he respected me. You couldn't tell her that though. I was so curious to find out what was going on with Kendra. I really loved my sister, and wanted things to be normal in her life. She was all I had, and I really learned to cherish her. So, I made a mental note to sit and talk with her when she got home from work, whether she was tired or not.

It was a little after 9 PM, and Kendra, was running later than usual. Normally, she would've been home and in bed by now. I arose from the couch and walked into the kitchen to get something to drink. As soon as I grabbed a cup from the kitchen cabinet, I heard noises coming from outside. There was a loud thump, and then what sounded to be a glass shattering. I immediately sat the cup on the kitchen counter before rushing over to the living room window to be nosey and see what all of the commotion was out front of my building.

"Stop it! Stop! Please stop!" I saw Kendra yelling, as Chris was dragging Kendra's boyfriend out of his car and beating him with what looked like…. A gun! I quickly opened the window and leaned out for a better view.

"Your bitch ass like beating women, huh!? How this feel mothafucka!" I heard Chris yelling, as he pistol whipped Kendra's boyfriend to a pulp. Blood was leaking out of his mouth, as Kendra, pled for Chris, to show him mercy. That is when I felt I had to intervene.

"Chris! Chris stop! Please bro, just let 'em be!" I yelled from the window, which made Chris come to a halt and look up towards me.

He instantly placed his pistol in his pocket, as if he didn't want me to see it, and released Kendra's boyfriend, from his grasp. Without saying another word, Chris, spit on Kendra's boyfriend, before walking down the street towards his house. Some older lady, whose name I later found out was Miss Johnson, comforted Kendra, as she stood on the sidewalk in shock, blaming herself.

"It's all my fault. I'm so sorry, it's all my fault." Kendra, cried aloud.

Miss Johnson, then escorted Kendra, into our building as her boyfriend, weakly, climbed himself into his car and slowly pulled off. Chris, damn near, beat the life out of him, and from what I now know, it was well deserved. I'm just glad Chris, didn't actually kill the man. Then I would've lost my only brother to the legal system. Seconds later, Kendra and Miss Johnson, walked into our apartment, and sat on the couch I was just sleeping on. By that time, I had ran in the bathroom and took a piss, before I met them in the living room. I stood there leaning on the wall, glancing out the window, as I listened to Miss Johnson and Kendra's conversation.

"Look'a here baby girl" Miss Johnson said to Kendra, as she stood up in front of Kendra and lifted her chin, demanding eye contact. "You are a beautiful young lady. Don't you ever let no man place his hands on you, you hear me?" Kendra then nodded her head in agreeance, as tears rolled down her cheeks. "It's not your fault! It's his fault, for not appreciating and respecting a woman of your stature. Now you gotta move on sweetie."

"But I really love him." Kendra cried.

"Baby girl, you got a heck of a lot to learn about life. Love is in the action, not the verbal. You showed him your love for him but did he show you the same? I never saw someone abuse what they love, whether mentally or physically. Take your time with love sweetheart, and get you some good rest tonight." Miss Johnson said, before kissing Kendra on the forehead and walking out the door.

I stood there, leaning on that wall in the living room, and watched my sister, Kendra, cry her heart out. Her eyes were puffy from the tears, but black and bruised from the beating her boyfriend gave to her. Kendra had scratch marks around her neck, as if she were choked, as well as reddish welts to confirm the grip. The more I stared at Kendra, the angrier I became. Now, it all started to make sense. I now understood why Kendra, became so distant from me. She didn't want me to see the pain she was going through. If it's anywhere close to the pain I feel right now after just watching my sister hurt, then I want her boyfriend to die. After tonight, my love and respect for Chris, grew a lot stronger and solid.

CHAPTER IV

"Derrick! Derrick! Wake up boy!" Kendra, frantically yelled, as she shook my shoulder.

"Wassup?" I yawned, as I stretched before I sat upward on my couch bed, giving Kendra, my full attention.

"Where's Chris? You need to go find him ASAP!" Kendra demanded, as she was walking into her bedroom.

I was still half sleep, but it felt as if I was still in a dream to be hearing Kendra interested in Chris' whereabouts.

It's been three days since the incident between Chris and Kendra's boyfriend. From what I read from the dude, he's far from the physical retaliation type so, I'm really, really, curious, as to what the urgency is. So, I quickly hopped out of bed and threw on my clothes and shoes, before walking into the bathroom to talk to Kendra.

"What's the problem with Chris?" I asked, Kendra, as she was damn near kissing the mirror as she perfected her makeup.

"Ralph, called and left a message, threatening to press charges on Chris, so you need to go tell him to lay low." Kendra spat, as she wiped her upper lip with a handkerchief, making sure her lipstick was neat.

"And who is Ralph?" I asked dumbfounded, still half sleep.

"My ex, dumb-dumb! Now go find him!" Kendra demanded, as she stormed past me into her bedroom as if she were in a rush to be somewhere.

"Aight, I be right back" I yelled to Kendra, as I rushed out of the front door of our apartment.

As I jetted out of our building and headed up the street towards Chris' house, I could see multiple police cruisers, crowding the street in front of Chris' house. When I got closer, I then saw police officers, walking out of Chris' house with Chris in their custody. He looked really calm and cool. I then saw, what I figured to be a detective, rise up out of the driver seat of an unmarked police cruiser, and walk towards Chris and the escorting officers, with his hand in a halt position, ordering them to stop in their tracks. He then grabbed Chris' arm and walked Chris over to the curb, where his police cruiser was parked. Holding Chris' arm with one hand, the detective looked into the backseat of his cruiser, before raising his free hand, giving a thumbs up as if he was awaiting a confirmation from someone who was seated there. The detective then nodded his head gesturing "yes" to the uniformed cops before they escorted Chris, to their police cruiser and placed him in the backseat. The detective, immediately, got into his cruiser and pulled off. As the car cruised past me, I got a glance into the backseat and to no surprise, it was Kendra's ex-boyfriend, Ralph. He attempted to duck low when our eyes locked in on each other, but by then it was too late. Seconds later, the remaining police cruisers drove past me. I then stared into the one that was escorting Chris. Chris, glanced over to me from the backseat. When our eyes caught contact, he then nodded his head with a smirk on his face, as if he was letting me know, he'll see me soon. I then smirked a little and gave him the thumbs up.

I immediately, ran back into the house to let Kendra know everything I just saw. She was in such a rush; all she could do was shake her head from left to right as if in shame. Without saying a word, she handed me a twenty-dollar bill and kissed me on the forehead before rushing out of the apartment. I wasn't sure if she was more so disappointed at Ralph getting Chris arrested, or at me losing a good friend who was like a brother to me. Maybe both! The one thing Chris did confirm, from the gesture on his face, was that I'll be seeing him again. And that was more than enough motivation for me to keep moving forward.

FLASHBACK

<u>**August 1991**</u>

"Don't do it son, please don't do it!" My dad pleaded, before I forcefully, pushed his wheelchair, causing him and the wheelchair to tumble down the wooden staircase of our home.

"You're sick, dad," I calmly said, as I walked down the staircase and stood over my father's lifeless body. "And momma misses you."

CHAPTER V

It's been a little over two years since Chris' arrest. Chris, was charged and convicted, of second-degree assault. The judge, sentenced him to 18 months, in prison, with three years, of supervised release, hanging over his head. At the time of the incident, I never knew that Chris, was already out on parole for a possession of a firearm case, in which he was already serving a three year, supervised release, parole sentence. He was only one year into that sentence. Chris served, 13 out of 18 months, including his good time, but wasn't released from prison because of a parole hold. When he finally got his chance to meet with the parole board, they decided to terminate that sentence after he first, served the remaining two years, in which he would still come home with another three years of parole over his head, because of Ralph, the rat.

One more year, and I'll get to kick it with my bro, Chris, again. With the help of Kendra, I've been sending Chris, letters, a little money, and pictures, whenever I get a chance to do so. Chris, was actually the one who convinced me into getting a part-time job to assist Kendra, in paying bills, as well as to help provide, food and clothing. On the weekends, I would work landscaping with this guy named, Victor. Victor, was a good friend of my mom before she died. He was a recovered addict, who hadn't smoked since my mother passed away. He said that her death opened his eyes. Victor, would always pay me one hundred dollars every weekend I worked. One hundred dollars, was nothing to most, but the world to me. Kendra, remained single for about a year or so, at least until she met, Black. Yeah, I said it… Black! Black, was as black as tar, and a thorough dude. He was a real live project product. He grew up, hung out and hustled around a neighborhood project called, *Potomac Gardens*, in Southeast. Black, was as cool as the breeze, but he smoked too much damn weed. Every time I looked up, he was smoking, and every time I turned around, Kendra, was cursing him out. Kendra, always found a reason to be mad at Black. And every time she would get fussy, all Black would do, is just laugh at her, or get up and leave out of the apartment. That alone would always make me laugh. The main reason I respected Black, was that no matter how angry or aggressive Kendra became, he never ever, ever, ever, ever even attempted to or gave any type of gesture as if he was gonna place a finger on

Kendra. Black, wasn't a small guy, and the gun he carried seemed bigger than me. I remember one day, Black, drove us to the *Safeway* grocery store, off of Minnesota Avenue and Benning Road, so that we could pick up some groceries. He was sitting in his car as usual, smoking and waiting for Kendra and me to come out of the store. When we finally did, there were a couple of dudes hanging in the parking lot. When we walked past them, they tried to push up on Kendra, and get her phone number. Kendra, ignored the guys and kept walking towards the car. That's when one of the dudes got angry and cursed at Kendra, calling her out of her name across the parking lot. Out of nowhere in a matter of seconds, Black, was out of the car with his pistol inside of that guys' mouth, in broad daylight. He then smacked the guy in the face with the pistol and forced him to apologize and call Kendra, a "Black Queen", before we sped off and headed back to the apartment. Kendra, was super mad at Black, for his actions, but little did he care. Black, was a man for respect. I really liked Black, and wished he could've stayed around, but he just couldn't stay out of jail. He was always getting arrested for something stupid and simple. One day he might say, "ride with me to take this piss test", then the next he saying, "ride with me to see my pretrial officer", then the next thing you know we're on our way to go get him an ankle monitor, then we're on our way to get it taken off. If it wasn't one thing, it was another, and Kendra, was fed up at it all. When she broke up with Black, he just shook my hand and left like he wasn't tripping about it at all. Black, looked unbothered. Honestly, I think Kendra did Black a favor, and on top of that, I was highly surprised when I had first met him. Surprised, that Kendra was actually dating a "real" black man. I think she was just experimenting and going through the motions of character transition. Kendra, was searching for her identity, and while experimenting, she was growing and understanding her tolerance as a woman. I respected the fact that she stepped outside of her norm. The way I see it, doing that only helps to grow your thoughts "outside of the box". Kendra, was growing as a woman, and in doing so, building her mental stability.

CHAPTER VI

On August 17, 2008, Chris, was finally released from prison. Right on time to place his vote for election. Chris, came home and showed his focus to establish himself. He was stacking money and doing really good for himself. The only flaw that Chris had, was the company that he kept. Chris, used to always keep this guy named, Flip, hanging around him, he wasn't with me. Chris and Flip, were obviously two totally different characters. They were like night and day. Flip had a dark soul. At the time, I wasn't sure if it was a matter of me not trusting Flip, or if I was just being jealous of Flip, for hanging with my brother more than me. At the end of the day, Chris, was living his life, and I was happy for him. I accepted Flip, only, because Chris, did.

It was very obvious that Chris had did a prison bid, because all he wanted to talk about was sports and politics. Before prison, it was money and Kendra. Even when Chris came home, he still had a crush on my sister, Kendra, but she was now married to this mulatto dude named, Jacob. Jacob, was a celebrity barber who everyone knew, and who knew everybody. And when I say everybody, I mean EVERYBODY! At the time, he was cutting A-Listers' hair such as Martin Lawrence, Dave Chappelle, and Gilbert Arenas. Jacob, was well known, throughout the, U.S. He was travelling all around the nation cutting hair and spent most of his time in California, with Martin, as well as a few other Hollywood celebrities. The way I saw it, Kendra, was more excited about his celebrity status than she was about him as a person. Jacob, was abusive. He never physically punched or slapped her, but once, he did choke her. He was a master of verbal abuse, and destroying Kendra's self-esteem. Kendra, submitted to him in arguments, especially, when he would threaten to leave or divorce her. Jacob, wasn't no fool. He knew his status and worth before getting married so, he convinced Kendra, into signing a prenup. I can't say that I blame him for that, especially, since she agreed to sign it. Being that there were so many gold diggers out here looking for any possible way to come up, the man had to protect his earnings. Little did he know, Kendra, was different. Though she was fond of Jacobs' status, Kendra, wasn't the type to care about a man's wealth, especially since she had been independent her entire life.

Kendra, was a true love seeker. She fell in love with Jacob, and though he was abusive, he was cool for the most part. Jacob, moved us out of that small apartment, into his mini mansion, in Potomac, Maryland. On top of that, he made sure that we kept the apartment, so that I could continue to finish school in DC. Some days, I would stay in the apartment throughout the week, to make sure I made it to school on time, and other days I would just ride back into the city with Kendra, on her commute to work. At the time, Kendra, was working for the federal government, in downtown DC, so, she would just drop me off at school, or the most convenient metro station, depending on her morning schedule.

After just two years of marriage, I finally understand why Jacob, really helped us keep that apartment, on Gault Place. So when he and Kendra, didn't work out, he'd easily have a place to send us to. And that's exactly what happened.
Jacob, had choked, Kendra, for the second, and last, time. Kendra was arrested for Assault with Intent to Kill, after she stabbed, Jacob, four times, and punctured a lung.

The charges were later dropped, after the government investigated the facts as well as with Jacob not pressing charges. Besides, they were still legally married at the time. Kendra lost her government job in the process, but immediately afterwards became employed at *Prime Time Investigations*, as a secretary. She was also a mentor to young girls for a non-profit organization. And of course, she continued to style hair on the side. We were making a living, and doing fine for ourselves, thanks to big sis.

June 2009, I graduated from *Spingarn Senior High School.* After seeing a black president in office, I was really inspired to attend college and received several offers from universities such as *Howard, James Madison, NC A&T*, and *Rutgers.* But, I wasn't motivated.

Chris, on the other hand, was making a great living off of driving eighteen wheelers. And I was highly interested in doing the same. I mean, he made it look good and tempting. Chris, was doing over the road driving. One day, he would call me from Arizona, or California, then the next day he would text me a picture from Montana somewhere. He was travelling, stacking money, and living life his way. So, I spent the summer of 2009, decision making. Analyzing, my future happiness. After my 18th birthday, in October, I decided to get my Class A CDL, and drive trucks. Being I wasn't over 21 yet, I wasn't eligible to drive interstate, only intrastate. January 2010, I finally obtained my Class A CDL, and though, I had lacked over the road experience, as most jobs required, Chris, was able to use a few of his connects and get me interviews set up from *Coca-Cola, UPS* and *FedEx*. I decided to work with *FedEx*. The money they offered as well as the schedule did me justice, especially, since I recently enrolled into the barbering school called, *Bennett Career Institute*. A few extra dollars wouldn't hurt none. I actually made a lot of money for my age, and was living a comfortable and stress free life.

CHAPTER VII

"Bro, I got my name changed back to Jones." Kendra, said to me as she picked up her purse from off the sofa.

"What took you so long?" I mumbled in sarcasm, which made Kendra, giggle, as we proceeded to walk out the front door of our apartment.

Being that I had just bought myself a silver 2006 Dodge Magnum R/T, about a week ago, I was always eager to drive. Kendra and I, climbed into my car and drove downtown to *Clyde's* restaurant. *Clyde's,* was an upscale restaurant, slash bar, which was connected to the *Verizon Center,* the home of the *Washington Wizards, Mystics* and *Capitals*. After being seated, a waitress took our orders before Kendra, got up and headed to the restroom. After about ten minutes, Kendra, came back to the table and sat down. A few seconds later, some white man walked up to our table with Kendra's identification, in his hand.

"Excuse me, ma'am. I think this belongs to you." The man said, with an Italian accent, as he handed Kendra, her I.D.

"Oh, thank you. I must've dropped it." Kendra replied, while batting her eyes at the man. You could clearly see that the man grew slightly nervous, because he immediately, darted his eyes towards me, in confusion.

"Oh, this is my little brother, Derrick." Kendra, quickly spat, to calm the guys' demeanor. His frown immediately turned into a smile.

"Oh okay." The man said, as he reached out to shake my hand. "It's nice to meet you Derrick, I'm Leo," he said, before looking at Kendra, and gently reaching for her hand. "And you are?"

"Oh I'm Kendra." My sister blushed, as she and Leo, stared into the gaze of each other's eyes.

"Well I'm sitting over here with a few co-workers of mine just having a drink. Just let me know if either of you need my services for anything." Leo said, before he smoothly walked back towards where he was seated.

"Seems like a nice guy." I said, to Kendra, who was still mesmerized as if she just saw the man of her dreams.

I mean, Leo, was a decent looking guy. A typical ladies man type. He stood about six feet tall, two hundred pounds solid, casually dressed with a tie. I would say he was no older than thirty-five, maybe. Plus, to top it off, he had his hair combed to the back like Zach, from *Saved By The Bell,* even though he looked more like AC Slater.

Honestly, if it weren't for his deep Italian accent, I would've thought that he was Samoan. He sounded like one of those mob guys that watch baseball all damn day and chew tobacco. After a fifteen minute wait, sipping water, and eating garlic bread, our food arrived. About five minutes into our meal, Leo, and his co-workers proceeded to leave, but not before saying his goodbyes.

"Well, back to the office I go. I hope to be seeing you two more often," Leo said, as he shook my hand, then Kendra's, as they once again, stared deeply into each other's eyes, as If they were reading one another's life story. "Are you two sure you don't need anything?"

"Yea, we're okay, thanks." I replied, as Leo, slightly unloosened his tie.

"Well in that case, you two make sure you enjoy your day peacefully." He replied, as he began to walk off.

"You too!" Kendra and I, replied in unison.

It took Kendra and I, about another ten minutes, to finish eating our meal, before Kendra, asked the waitress for the check. That's when the waitress handed Kendra, a receipt with writing on the back of it. It read;

LEO 202-555-6080

HOPE TO HEAR FROM YOU SOON

"The bill was taken care of." The waitress said, as she collected our plates, glasses, and silverware, from off the table.

"Well then, I got a tip for you then," Kendra replied, while digging inside of her purse.

"Thanks, but no thanks, ma'am. The mister took care of that also." The waitress replied, with a smile. "You two enjoy your day. My name is Cindy. You can ask for me anytime you come back here." Cindy said, before walking off.

I then looked at Kendra, as she stared at me and shrugged her shoulders, before we both smiled and walked out of the restaurant.

"You gonna call him?" I asked Kendra, as we climbed into my car.

"Should I?" she replied, with a smile on her face, patiently waiting to hear my response.

That's when I started the ignition and placed on my seatbelt, before staring at Kendra, shaking my head up and down. I gave her the approval she sought.

"When we get home sis." I instructed, confirming my approval, before pulling out of the parking space, on our way home.

I haven't seen Kendra smile like this in a while. I mean, she was glowing with relief. That glow, left me no choice, but to approve. Kendra, deserved happiness.

CHAPTER VIII

Just like that, Kendra, was married again. She and Leo, went to the *District of Columbia Marriage Bureau,* after just nine months of dating, with plans of having a real wedding during the summer of, 2012. Kendra and Leo, were living in a single family home in Northwest, on 16th Street. Kendra, Leo, and his daughter Sarah, of course. At the time, Sarah, was only thirteen years young. Leo and Sarah's mom, Cynthia, were married for seven years, before her mom went missing just four years ago, while she and Leo, were on a vacation in Aruba, celebrating their anniversary. Still, to this day, no sign of her. No motives, no suspects, no witnesses, no body, nothing! Just another unsolved mystery. Sarah, attached herself to Kendra from the first day she met her, and Kendra, happily took on the responsibility of being Sarah's mom. I mean, they were inseparable.

Kendra's life, was picture perfect, and I was so happy to see her happy. So happy, I even once overlooked the random bruise on her bicep, complimented, with a black eye. When I asked, Kendra, about the wounds, she just lied and made obvious excuses before redirecting our conversation elsewhere. She then, later told me, "No matter what Leo and I go through, you just stay out of it and mind your business. We're a married couple, bro, and we need to learn how to work things out." BULLSHIT! I thought to myself. See I was young and sometimes naïve, but I wasn't no fool. Kendra, was my big sister so, I always respected her wishes, even when I didn't agree with them. So, I did my best in trying to mind my own business. Sis, knew what was best for her. So I thought!

CHAPTER IX

I was still working my job at *FedEx,* and stacking up my money for a rainy day. I was still living in that same apartment on Gault Place, paying little to nothing for the rent, and I was still single. I just couldn't find the right one. Maybe, because I was still young, energetic, and getting money, or maybe it was because I had front row seats into Kendra's life and relationships. Chris, once told me that he's never settling down. He said, "All this grass on the field and you talking about sitting on the bench." That quote alone, made me never talk about finding a girlfriend, to Chris again. He was who I looked up to so, I felt silly even discussing the thoughts of a girlfriend.

Whenever Chris, wasn't working, we were partying and mingling with all types of women from all types of nationalities. A lot of them had girlfriend potential, at least until they drank alcohol. That's when my entire perspective about them would instantly change. Our life was turnt up! Outside of my job, I used to help Kendra, run her beauty & barbershop, she opened on H Street, in Northeast. I helped with the bookkeeping but would mostly treat it as a side job and cut a few of the clients' hair, as well as manage and supervise the other barbers that were there. I would also help clean up the shop and sometimes close it up. Lately, I've been noticing a drastic change in Kendra's features, attitude, and health choices, which made me come to the shop more often than usual to keep a close eye on her. I mean, she's been running back and forth to the restroom on the hour, to suddenly vomiting in a trash can, had me wondering, what in the hell Leo, had been poisoning my sister with? I was really concerned. I know she told me to stay out of her and Leo's business, but it was a necessity that I figured out what was going on. I loved my sister, Kendra, dearly with all of my heart and other than Chris, she's all I have and can depend on in this world.

"Derrick, can you lock up the shop for me please?" Kendra, asked me as she started stuffing things inside of her purse, getting ready to leave out of the shop. "I gotta run and go to a business meeting with Leo."

"Yea, I got you." I replied, as I grabbed the broom and started sweeping the floor. "I ain't got much to do anyway."

"Thanks bro." Kendra replied, as she attempted to walk out of the shop.

"Aye sis." I said, stopping Kendra, before she walked out.

"Yeah, what's up bro?" Kendra replied, from the doorway with a concerned look on her face.

"Aye sis, um, I've been kinda noticing you've been sick a lot lately." I said nervously, not trying to offend Kendra in the process. "I mean, I'm just a little concerned about your health, that's all."

Unexpectedly, Kendra smiled, with the puppy dog eyes.

"Aww... my little brothers' concerned about his big sister, how sweet." Kendra replied, with a giggle. "Derrick, I'm pregnant... love you brother." Kendra said, with a huge smile on her face before walking out of the door.

I was left standing in the middle of the shop, with my under armpit leaning on that broom stuck in awe. I didn't know what to say or how to react. I was surprised, but at the same time, filled with joy, from the news I just received. After about three minutes, I sat down in one of the barber chairs and exhaled, before coasting into a deep thought. I thought about all that was needed to be done to help raise a child. I'm about to be an uncle! So excited, but nervous. The butterflies that floated in the pit of my stomach were uncontrollable. I was ready to jump up and scream out of excitement, but instead I once again exhaled. After gathering my thoughts, I quickly finished cleaning the shop and closed it up, before calling Chris, to pinpoint his whereabouts. Times like this made for only one thing. A CELEBRATION!

CHAPTER X

"Congratulations!" I yelled to Kendra, as I stepped towards her bedside joyfully viewing her newborn baby boy, Dominion. "I'm an uncle." Is what I had whispered to Kendra, as she wiped the tear drops from her eyes with her right hand while cradling baby Dominion with her left arm.

Resting with his eyes closed, he was wrapped up inside of a blanket like an eggroll. Dominion, had a head full of hair and rosy red cheekbones, looking just like his father, Leo, just spit him out. Usually, babies would grow into their features, but not Dominion. He came straight out of the womb looking exactly like his daddy.

> "He looks like my pops" Leo said, as he walked into the room with a paper bowl full of fruit cocktail and bottles of apple juice, orange juice, and *Aquafina*, water. "You need to eat, baby." Leo, whispered to Kendra, as he sat the items on to a nearby table.

He then, walked over to the sink to wash his hands, before receiving Dominion, from Kendra, cradling him in his arms, as he sat in a chair by the window. I then, retrieved the fruit cocktail and beverages, from the table and handed them to Kendra.

> "Wow," Leo, whispered in amazement to Dominion. "You look so much like your grandpa."

From what Kendra, told me, Leo's dad, was murdered, when Leo, was thirteen years young, and his mom had committed suicide, exactly one year prior. Leo, was a foster child for most of his juvenile life, in which he bounced from home to home, as well as did a small bid inside of a juvenile residential center slash prison. You could never guess from looking at Leo, that he suffered so much trauma and pain as a juvenile. Leo, was really private about his past life, but from the looks of things, he never let it stop or hinder him from being great. Leo, was a mild mannered, career and family oriented man, who carried himself with respect. My only beef with him was his minor abuse towards Kendra. It wasn't something that happened often, but it did happen once, and once was enough for me. Due to Kendra's wishes, I chose not to ever mention anything about it to Leo, nor show any signs that I was aware. I just played it cool and played the dumb role, at least for now. I just pray that it doesn't happen again. I'm not sure how cool I can be then.

"So Derrick, what's the plans for tonight?" Leo, asked me as he rocked baby Dominion, back and forth.

"Not sure," I said, while scrolling through my phone. "I was supposed to be linking up with Chris, and slide over to The Stadium night club for a New Year's Eve party, but I ain't heard nothing from bro yet."

Surprisingly, no missed calls, no texts, NOTHING! That was highly unusual. Usually, Chris would've hit my phone by now.

"BRO YOU GOOD?" I texted to Chris' phone, impatiently awaiting a reply.

> "I'll be right back, y'all." I said, while walking towards the room entrance. "I'ma go out here and hit Chris' phone real quick."

> "Yea bro, 'cause it's pretty late." Kendra replied, as I walked out of the room into the lobby of the hospital, and flopped into one of the sofa chairs.

I then, called Chris' phone several times, in which the calls went straight to voicemail.

> "Chris, what the fuck." I mumbled, aloud to myself, as my mind raced, wondering where Chris, could be.

The clock on my phone read, 12:27 AM. It was the first day of January, 2012, and I've spent my New Year's Eve, inside a hospital, with Kendra, and Leo. Dominions', birth time was clocked in at 12:02 AM, shortly after everyone in the hospital was yelling, "HAPPY NEW YEARS!" to one another.

Usually by now, I would've received a text or call from Chris, saying, 'HAPPY NEW YEARS', but nothing. Optimistically thinking, he's laid up somewhere with a dime piece, having the time of his life, I'm sure. Well, maybe next year it'll be better for us. Honestly, if Chris, would call me now talking about partying, I would have to decline. I'm exhausted, due to all of the drama that came along with the beauty of birth. Anticipation is mind draining. So, I eventually decided to head home to rest. After saying my goodbyes to Kendra, Leo, and Dominion, I rushed out of the hospital and sped home, chasing my bed.

En route, I've tried calling Chris' phone several times, but still no answer. When I pulled in front of my apartment building, it was surprisingly empty on the block. All I saw was a police cruiser, sitting across the street, in the alleyway beside, *Mount Vernon Church*. As usual, I figured the police might have ruined the party, which forced everybody either to the club or inside someone's house. Regardless, I was too tired to participate. My mind was so excited about the baby, Dominion, also. After rushing into my apartment, I quickly undressed before damn near diving into my bed, eager to rest up for the upcoming future. It was a new year, a new day, and a new beginning, that I looked forward to exploring.

CHAPTER XI

"Damn, I was out of it." I said to myself, as I stretched, before climbing out of my bed to get my day started.

I then, looked at my, *iPhone 4S*, and the clock on it read, 11:07 AM. I must've been super sleepy, because that was the first time in over two years that I had slept more than six hours.

"Twelve missed calls?" I mumbled to myself, as I walked into the bathroom and brushed my teeth.

The entire time I spent brushing my teeth, I wondered, what was so important for me to have twelve missed calls? I mean, I barely get one. Well, whatever it was would have to wait to be discussed after I grab a bowl of cereal. I was starving.

After I prepped myself a bowl of cereal, I sat on my living room sofa and started checking all of my messages. I saw I had text messages from Kendra, as well as Miss Johnson, saying, *"CALL BACK ASAP!"* I also, had four voicemail messages, which I rarely get. And to make matters worse, no missed calls, or messages from Chris. I hope all is well with him. As I scrolled through my phone to return Kendra and Miss Johnsons' calls, I heard a bunch of yelling and crying, outside of my front window. That's when I arose from the couch and walked over to the window to peek out of the blinds. What I saw was a few guys and females that live and hang on the block, drinking liquor, and consoling each other. First and foremost, it was too damn early to be drinking liquor, and secondly, where the hell is Chris?

CLACK! CLACK! CLACK! Was the sound I heard, as someone was knocking on the front door of my apartment. I first, rushed back into the kitchen to sit down my bowl of cereal, on the kitchen counter, before I hurried to the front door and glanced through the peephole. It was Miss Johnson, on the other side.

"Gimme a second, Miss Johnson!" I yelled, as I ran into my bedroom, to dress myself in some jeans and a tee shirt. Usually, I'm walking around my home in just my underwear. I'm not used to having company over, plus, I'm just really getting my ass out of bed. After getting dressed, I rushed over to the front door to see Miss Johnson, standing on the other side of it with a devastating look on her face. Her eyes looked so drained, as if she had cried them drier than the *Sahara Desert*, but she also looked as if she was about to start back crying again. I then, stepped to the side, welcoming, Miss Johnson, inside. As she walked into my apartment, Miss Johnson, reached her arms out towards me before we embraced each other with a hug. That's when Miss Johnson, burst into tears. I reached out and pushed the door closed with one of my hands, before escorting, Miss Johnson, over to the sofa to have a seat, as she cried harder and harder, by the second.

"Why in the devil is everyone so darn shiesty!?" Miss Johnson, wept. "This madness just needs ta' stop in the name of Jesus!"

I just sat there on the sofa, quiet and confused, as to what Miss Johnson was referring to, as I held her in my arms and listened to her vent. After about ten minutes, Miss Johnson, settled down. That's when I got up and went to the kitchen and poured her a glass of water. When I came back, I sat down beside her and handed her the glass of water as she attempted to wipe away the small river of tears that covered her face.

"You okay, Miss Johnson?" I asked, which made her nod her head up and down, gesturing yes, as she sniffled while taking a sip of the water. "Are you ready to talk about it?" I asked, which alarmed Miss Johnson, who looked up into my eyes with a look on her face which showed sorrow and disbelief.

Miss Johnson, then slowly shook her head from left to right.

"You don't know, do you?" Miss Johnson said, with a cracked up voice, as if she was afraid to ask me the question.

That's when I became alert, as my eyes enlarged, my blood began to rush, and my heart rate sped up as my mind raced, cancelling out each and every negative thought I figured I wasn't prepared to mentally handle.

"Know what, Miss Johnson?" I nervously asked, out of confusion and fear.

"Poor baby." Miss Johnson replied, as she sat down the glass of water on the floor beside the couch before tightly embracing me in her arms, as if she were stabilizing me like a straitjacket. "Baby I'm so sorry," Miss Johnson whispered, "Last night, Chris was murdered."

CHAPTER XII

Six days passed, and I've been laying around this house weeping. I badly needed a haircut before Chris' funeral, tomorrow. So, I forced myself together and dragged myself around the corner to *Life Style Barber Shop*, on Minnesota Avenue. This past week, I've learned a lot more in detail about Chris', homicide, but nobody really understood why it happened. I mean, how can you understand when Chris, was murdered by his right hand man, Flip. I'm guessing we're all finally learning one of the reasons why his nickname was Flip. Besides myself, Flip was the only other person Chris genuinely trusted. I was informed that they were all outside hanging on Gault Place, drinking and partying with a few females who worked at the strip club, before Chris and Flip, walked off together into the alleyway beside *Mount Vernon Church*, to let off their guns for the New Year's Day Celebration, which is a natural hood tradition in the United States.

Word on the streets was that when Chris, started bussing his gun into the air, Flip, upped his pistol, and shot Chris in his head, one time. The lead detective on the case said, forensic determined the same exact thing. The very few people that heard from Flip, say that Flip, is now trying to promote "self-defense". A smart defense, but dumb! Why!? That's the main question everyone's been asking. Everyone who knows Chris, knows that he would never in his life attempt to kill Flip, or nobody that he considered a close friend or family member. But on the other hand, everyone who knows Flip, knows that he's known to have a little rattlesnake in his blood. He once in the past robbed his everyday hanging partner, Fat Eddy. See Fat Eddy, was a non-violent type of guy. The last thing Fat Eddy wanted, was problems. He was just a true hustler at heart. At least, before Flip, came in his house and robbed him for all of his drugs and money. Eighteen ounces of hard rock, 200 ecstasy pills, and forty-five thousand, in cash. Not to mention, Fat Eddy's two handguns, in which he had no intentions of ever using. After the robbery, nobody ever saw Fat Eddy on Gault Place, ever again. Last I heard, was that Fat Eddy, went and got himself a government job.

A lot of people used to question and wonder why Chris, would let Flip, be near his presence. It was like night and day. But Chris, was different than everybody else. He wasn't the type that would judge a person based on their past actions. He once told me, "We all make mistakes. It's how you right your wrongs that define the man." Chris, saw the good in everyone. So when he gravitated to you, you knew it. And if he grew to hate you, you damn sure knew that too. Chris, had no gray areas. Actually, it took a lot for Chris to grow hate for someone. You pretty much had to be a real live scumbag, or a snitch, or an advantage-taker for Chris to really hate you. Flip, was highly manipulative, and perpetrated as if he was an honorable man. As if he grew, and changed from his old ways. And that's how he got up under Chris. At one point in time, Flip, was a ghost in Chris' eyes. I mean, the two never shared a conversation before Chris went off to prison. I was wondering how they became so buddy, buddy, after Chris came home from prison. So, one day I decided to ask Chris about their relationship, and he explained it all to me. Chris, told me that when he and Flip were locked up together over DC Jail, they got into a slight beef with a few dudes from over the Trinidad neighborhood. It was more so Chris' problem, which had stemmed over the pay phone. Chris said, he began fighting about five or six dudes, before Flip, ran to his aid. Though, they were outnumbered, they handled their own and went out swinging. Flip, got stabbed in his shoulder for Chris, and that's how Flip gained a lot of respect and love from

Chris, which is highly understandable. Only the realest individuals would stay tight with a person who went to war for them, and to me, Chris was the realest. This outcome was destined. Chris, as a man, did exactly what he was supposed to do, and that's be loyal to all that has proven theirs. It's impossible to know that loyalty and betrayal, would one day produce a baby. It was impossible for him to know that that knife puncture that Flip took in the shoulder, would someday be returned as a gunshot wound to the head. And neither did I....

As I bent the corner on the side of *Big D,* liquor store, on Minnesota Avenue, I saw police cruisers pulling off from in front of *Life Style Barber Shop*, as well as two detectives walking out of the barbershop.

> "Again, we apologize for all of the commotion outside of your shop, sir, and you take it easy." I heard one of the detectives say to the owner of the barber shop, before climbing inside of the passenger seat of his unmarked police cruiser, as his partner swiftly pulled off.

I then, walked into the barbershop and had a seat in the waiting area before my designated barber, Bee-Love, called my name as he waved me over to his chair. "Right on time," I thought to myself. In and out.

"Aye Dee, you saw that nigga out there?" Bee-Love asked me, as I sat in his chair.

"Saw who, bruh?" I replied.

"Flip bitch ass."

"Nah, where he at?" I asked, with a stomach full of butterflies.

The sound of his name made my stomach cringe.

"He was out front posted up chilling for about five minutes, then them undercovers came out of nowhere," Bee-Love, dramatically explained, as he pointed toward the front of the shop. "This dumb ass nigga was posted right here on this busy ass avenue, like he was tryna get caught or something. Like it ain't twenty-five thousand dollar wanted posters hanging around everywhere." Bee-Love joked.

"Shit crazy." I mumbled, as I shook my head from left to right, in disbelief as to what Bee-Love was explaining to me.

The entire time Bee-Love cut my hair, he joked about how dumb and stupid Flip was. Everybody that was in the shop at the time, joked about all of the dumb shit that Flip has done throughout the years, and we all came to the agreeance, that Chris, was Flip's, guardian angel. If it wasn't for Chris' presence, Flip, would've been doing either a life sentence in prison, or in his grave. Then the dummy kills his angel. How ironic!

I've learned a lot from this situation. Though, it tremendously hurts my soul, I got a gut feeling that one day this experience would save my life. Chris, was also my guardian angel, but I also believe that he was my sacrificial lamb for my future experiences, which are yet to be seen.

CHAPTER XIII

HEY NEPHEW,

YOUR SISTER TOLD ME ABOUT YOUR HOMEBOY CHRIS. I'M SORRY TO HEAR ABOUT THAT. I NEVER GOT A CHANCE TO MEET HIM, BUT FROM WHAT I HEARD, HE WAS A SOLID, STAND-UP GUY. A FEW OF MY YOUNGINS IN HERE SPEAK HIGHLY OF HIM. LET ME KNOW IF YOU EVER NEED SOMEONE TO TALK TO OR JUST WRITE ME ANYWAY. I'VE READ SOMEWHERE THAT WRITING IS THERAPEUTIC, AND HONESTLY, IT'S HELPED ME GET THROUGH THIS PRISON SENTENCE. SPEAKING OF THAT, YOU KNOW I'M FINALLY ON MY LAST LAPS. ONLY A FEW YEARS LEFT, THEN I'M OUTTA HERE. WE CAN GO TO SOME OF THOSE REDSKINS AND WIZARDS GAMES SOON'S I TOUCH DOWN. I'VE BEEN STAYING OUT THE WAY, SO I'M

PRETTY SURE THE PAROLE BOARD SHOULD BE GIVING ME SOME PLAY. MAKE SURE YOU WRITE ME BACK NEPHEW AND I'LL KEEP IN TOUCH AND CHECK ON YOU. SEND MY LOVE TO KENDRA AND THE BABY. LOVE YOU BIG GUY.

SINCERELY,
UNCLE MIKE

I can't wait to see my uncle Mike. He surely always seems to reach out right on time. My uncle Mike was my mother's friend. Actually, he was a close friend of the family long before Kendra and I were born. So, he was more so like a brother to my mom and pops. Uncle Mike, always looked after us, and made sure we had things such as food and clothing. He went to prison for murder, back in '96 when I was a child. I heard that Uncle Mike went nuts in prison after my mothers' death. Rumor has it that nobody was safe. He allegedly beat up prison guards, stabbed several other inmates, and spent majority of his time locked down in the hole, or what they called the SHU! My mom was pretty much all that Uncle Mike had left on the streets. After his arrest, Uncle Mikes' entire bloodline was killed in a murder spree, in what the newspaper headlined as *"THE SIX MONTH RAIN FORECAST"*. For the whole six months, it was raining bullets. Not only that, people were buried alive, cemented in bedroom closets, and a couple were decapitated. 71 people were shot and 14 murdered in the 7th ward, all within a six month span, and not one conviction. Amazing! There was nothing the police could do to stop it. Word on the streets, was that my uncle Mike, killed the wrong guy. And from what I've heard from a few older guys, is that they highly doubt the fact that my uncle Mike, is done retaliating. Kendra and I, were the last line of sanity Uncle Mike had to hold onto, and from his consistent communication, he's proven that he's here for us no matter what. So, we made sure that we were there for him, unconditionally.

It's been over a week since Chris' funeral, and I've already went back to work. I can't say I was in my highest spirits as usual, but I've been keeping it cordial. Honestly, if it weren't for the joy of my nephew, Dominion, I'd possibly be still laying up in the bed mourning. Dominion, represented my strength. He was a soul savior. Hope!

*Phone Ringing*

"What's up, sis, how you?" I said to Kendra, into the receiver, as I folded Uncle Mike's letter and put it back into the envelope.

"What you doing?" Kendra asked, from the other side of the phone.

"Nothing, really. Just was reading the letter Uncle Mike wrote to me. I'm done now, though."

"Well good! Guess what the hell I just found out!?" Kendra said, sounding surprised.

"What!?"

"You remember Ralph?"

"Who the hell is that?"

"My ex-boyfriend. The one Chris went to jail for."

"Oh yeah, the geeky dude. Wassup wit slim?"

"They locked his ass up, that's what's up!"

"What he do, some credit card scamming or something?" I joked.

"Oh, you wouldn't believe this shit!!!!"

"What!?"

"This son of a bitch, got arrested for Conspiracy to Murder."

"What the hell he been doing? What he kill, a fly?" I joked.

"Nope! He's supposedly the one who got Chris killed."

"WHAT!" I yelled into the phone, surprised from what I just heard but more so confused as to whether Kendra was accurate with her information or not.

"Yep! The news saying he placed a twenty-thousand dollar bounty on Chris, and Flip took the hit." Kendra explained, sounding frustrated.

"What the hell!"

"Yep! And the news saying Flip is cooperating against Ralph."

"Damn." I replied, as I shook my head from left to right.

Kendra and I, conversed on the phone for at least another fifteen minutes, before hanging up. The whole time we talked, I was in a daze. All I could really say was, ""What!" and "What the hell!" I really couldn't believe the info I was hearing. Honestly, if it wasn't coming from Kendra's mouth, I wouldn't have believed it until I saw it myself. And Flip on the other hand…. So gangster and shiesty, but quick to snitch. One thing I've learned about a snake, is he don't got a backbone. So being surprised, is something I should not be. Betrayal is in Flips' genetics, whether it's for the American dollar or for his freedom. He's a snake!

I've never in my life been the violent and aggressive type of person, but at this point, if I would ever see Flip or Ralph, I'm pretty sure I would murder them both in cold blood. I mean, Chris was like my brother. My only brother. He helped in the development of my manhood. He and Kendra, and her gift to life, baby Dominion. I just pray that they both outlive me, because without either of them, I fear I will become something unrighteous.

CHAPTER XIV

For the past year, I've been attending all of Ralph's court dates. And from the look of things, he's soon expected to take a plea offer from the government. I was also making appearances at Raymond Edwards', also known as Flip, court appearances, until the judge ordered him to have closed court proceedings. Flips' attorney argued how they feared for his safety, and the prosecution agreed. At every one of his court dates, there were at least a group of five different sets of men and women, sitting in the audience, heckling Flip. That lasted for about three court appearances until one day, the U.S. Marshals ordered everyone other than the attorneys, legal representation, and court officials, out of the courtroom. That was the last of what we saw of Flip. It was no mystery that Flip was planning to testify on Ralph. That alone, on top of him murdering a well-loved and respected individual, totaled up to a life of hell in prison.

On another note, this past year hasn't mentally, been on my side. From all of the mourning I've been doing, I wound up getting myself laid off from my job. I've been missing days left and right. Luckily, I have a Class-A CDL, which made finding another job a given, even though I was not in a rush to get back to work. Honestly, I think I've gotten lazy, due to everything that was happening in my life as well as in Kendras'. I was mentally drained. And Leo's constant drama was not helping. His respect for Kendra seemed as if it were slowly fading, and it was noticeable. President Obama, once again winning the election was probably the only good news I remember hearing within the past year. Hopefully, that was a good sign that this year would be by far better than the last.

I was actually contemplating whether or not I should hit the streets of DC tonight, to celebrate the presidents' inauguration. During the previous inauguration, there were over three million people, flooded throughout the streets of DC. Only lord knows how many people will show up this time around. This might be the last time we get to see a black president win a presidential race, so why not go out and enjoy history. Hopefully, when I have kids and grandkids, I can share with them this once in a lifetime experience. And if I'm unlucky with having children, then I can always share my experiences with my nephew, Dominion, and his kids. So I decided to take myself a shower and get dressed.

"Damn, that shower felt good." I mumbled to myself as I walked into the kitchen in just my boxer briefs, to get a cup of water.

For some reason, hot showers always dehydrated me.

Phone ringing

"Damn!" I exclaimed to myself, as I detoured toward the bedroom to retrieve my cell phone, which I had left laid on my bed. *LEO,* was the name that was displayed on the screen. I tapped the *TALK* icon.

"Hello." I spoke into the phone.

"Hey Derrick!" Leo frantically said into the phone.

"What's up, Leo. What's the problem?" I asked, as I sat onto the edge of my bed, feeling uncomfortable with the tone of Leo's voice.

"It's about Kendra, bro." Leo nervously whispered.

"Okay!" I aggressively replied.

"She's on her way to the hospital, bro. I'm following the ambulance as we speak."

"Why? What the fuck happened!?"

"She was running to grab Dominion, before he crawled down the stairs, and slipped and tumbled down the steps. I think she's suffering a concussion, bro."

"Damn! How's Dominion!?"

"Dom is fine. She actually didn't get a chance to pick him up before tripping up."

"Damn, that's crazy!" I exclaimed, before placing my phone on speaker and laying it on the bed. "Which hospital y'all headed to?"

"They said we're going to GW."

"Aight then, I'll see you soon." I replied, while quickly putting on my clothes.

"Okay brother, drive safe." Leo said, before ending out call.

If it ain't one thing, it's another. Looks like my plans for tonight are cancelled, and honestly, I'ma take that as a sign of life. Maybe it wasn't meant for me to go out tonight. Also, I was thinking that it's about that time for me to be getting back to work. I've been out of work long enough, and with Kendra having concussions and the drama amongst her and Leo, I'm pretty sure that she will soon need me for aid and assistance so, me stacking cash is my current priority. Not just for me and Kendra, but for the baby, Dominion. I need to help prepare for my nephews' future. Life is short. If anything was to ever happen to my sister, Kendra or I, at least Dominion, wouldn't have a financial burden. He would be good. And if he's good, then I'm great!

CHAPTER XV

<u>August 1, 2013</u>

The past six months have been productive for me, but it's also been mentally draining. I managed to get myself back to work, driving for *Coca-Cola*, making 70k a year plus a five thousand dollar signing bonus. I've also disciplined myself to save at least two thousand dollars a month, and have been consistent with meeting that quota. My spending habits tremendously declined, and I've been spending a lot more time inside of my home and with, Dominion. I've made myself a goal, and stuck to it. Also, back in April, Ralph, accepted a plea agreement to a 240 month prison sentence for conspiring to murder, Chris. Flip, was also sentenced to 240 months in prison, even though he attempted to become a rat for the government.

They still threw his ass to the wolves and that's when I understood and realized how much the government really cared about their cooperators. Worthless! Besides that, the only thing that has been bothering me was Kendra's situation. In the past six months, Kendra, has been hospitalized four times. Concussions, a broken wrist, bruises, black eyes… and all I could do was watch. Kendra made excuse, after excuse, after excuse, for Leo. I even sent Miss Johnson, to sit down and talk to Kendra, and she boldface lied to her just to protect Leo's honor. She was morally saving his face value, while he was physically destroying hers. Since that first hospital visit, when Kendra allegedly fell down the stairs, I've despised Leo, and he knew it. That day, the doctor stood right in front of us and said, "It doesn't look as if she just fell down the stairs because there were no other bruises on her body that would indicate a fall." The doctor also said, "She either bumped her head on something really hard on something solid, or someone delivered a harsh blow to her head." I sat and watched Leo stumble over his words as he tried to explain what happened to Kendra to the doctor as well as police officers. Every time he recited it, he became more confident in his story, and was starting to believe it himself. A good liar to deaf ears, but I was listening. And I wasn't buying it. Now, Leo, got my mind racing. He got me doing things out of my character. Like thinking of ways to make him disappear without harming Kendra's heart. Strategic and smart is how I have to move, but quick and precise, before it's too late.

CHAPTER XVI

November 2013

"Bro, Eric is the coolest. He had slid through my job and brought me lunch, plus he's very, very respectful. He's been a good friend, and he respects my marriage. I wish I could've met him before Leo." Kendra said to me, over the phone.

She was referring to my homeboy, Eric, who used to work with me at my old *FedEx* job. Eric, was a real cool, laidback and classy guy. Church going, but he spent a lot of his time on the road now driving for *Walmart*. He was an eligible bachelor. No kids, never married, and God-fearing. High yellow, tall and clean cut. He was a sincere person as well. Eric and Kendra, have been good friends ever since I introduced them to each other a few weeks ago at my birthday party. Honestly, I think Kendra, communicates with Eric, even more than I do. And every time he's back in town from a road trip, they hook up and spend time with one another. Sometimes, Leo, would call my phone, asking me if I'd heard from Kendra, and I would already have a lie waiting for him. Then I would inform Kendra on the lie I told him, so she could be on point. I could tell he was getting curious, and growing suspicion, but who cares. I was planning to make him vanish once and for all. His presence was useless. Besides, I felt like I was pretty much raising Dominion, anyway. My nephew, spent more time with me than he did with Kendra and Leo put together. My first thought in my elimination plan was to send a female friend of my choice to flirt and hookup with Leo, before getting him caught up by Kendra, and force a divorce, but I then had to reevaluate that. He'd just manipulate her like he always does, into taking him back. Any woman who's foolish enough to allow someone to beat her half to death, could care less about her spouse cheating. That was the least of her worries. So, I concluded with myself, that the only way to get rid of Leo, was to really get rid of Leo. Especially while Kendra was so caught up in Eric. Her feelings for him were growing rapidly, which made now the perfect time to execute my plan of execution. I didn't need Kendra to feel the full effects of this transition.

CHAPTER XVII

"Hey sis, can I use your car?" I asked Kendra, while she was leaning over inside the sink, washing one of her client's hair at the salon. "I've been ducking this lil' broad, and I don't want her to see my car. I gotta run to the house real quick."

"Boy, you simple." Kendra giggled, while shaking her head from left to right. Kendra, had always gotten a good laugh out of my women affairs, or "shenanigans", as she used to say.

"For real though, sis. I'ma leave you my car keys. I'll be back before you finish drying her hair." I replied, as I handed Kendra, my set of keys.

"Put them in my bag over there and get mine out." Kendra said, as she nodded her head, signaling me to where her purse was located.

"You still got a copy of my apartment key on here?" I asked, as I removed her set of keys from out of her purse.

"Of course. Yours is the blue tape and mine is the red."

"Oh, so you set tripping, huh?" I joked aloud, which caused Kendra as well as all the other women inside of the salon to laugh.

"Boy, bye!" Kendra exclaimed while laughing, as I exited the salon.

I always left the women in the salon with something to gossip about. Most women hate men, and I understand this. So, when I say or do something bogus, it always leaves a door open for them to start thinking negatively and point their fingers at every man in the world, as if we all have the same social security number. We're considered dogs, and to us, they're a bunch of sneaky pussycats.

It took me no time to get to *Deane Avenue Cleaners,* on Nannie Helen Burroughs Avenue in Northeast. I've been coming to this spot since I was a youngin', back when Kendra was employed here as a teenager, so I was known on a first name basis. It took me no time to get to Kendra's house key cloned, so I decided to treat her to a meal.

PHONE RINGING

"What boy?" Kendra said into the phone.

"You hungry?" I asked Kendra, as I sat in the car, while parked in the parking lot of the cleaners.

"Ain't I always?" Kendra joked, which forced me to laugh. "Where you eating at?"

"I was about to go pull up on Dreko and Ty Stunna, over at *MLK Deli* and holla at them real quick. Get you one of those crab cakes."

"Yeesss! Them jo'nts be like that." Kendra agreed excitedly. Shrimp and crabs were Kendra's favorite food.

"Aight, I'm 'bout to call over there. I be back soon."

"Okay then, bro." Kendra said before hanging up.

PHONE RINGING

"*MLK Deli*." The voice on the other side of the line said.

"Who this, Dre?" I asked.

"Wassup, bob, this Derrick, right?" Dre replied, in question.

"Yeah, bruh. How you slim?"

"I'm cooling. What you tryna eat playa?"

"No homo fool. Let me get two glizzy's, no homo, and a half pound crab cake demonstration."

"Aight, so you said you want two of them jo'nts, huh?" Dre joked, which made us both laugh simultaneously.

"No homo." I replied.

"Aight bob, you on your way?" Dre asked.

"Yeah fool. I be there in 'bout ten minutes.

"Aight then, bet. Your total is thirty-four dollars and ninety cents." Dre replied, as I heard him hitting buttons on a cash register. "Your no homos should be ready by the time you get here." Dre joked.

"Aight bruh, I'm gone." I said laughing, before hanging up the phone.

It took me no more than ten minutes to get over to *MLK Deli* to pick up my order. Another fifteen minutes later, I was pulling up in front of Kendra's salon in Northeast. I drove in silence the entire ride. No music, no radio, no nothing. I was too busy caught up in my thoughts, analyzing the best way to make Leo disappear without any repercussions. The sweetest joy of revenge. Revenge, for all that he has done to Kendra. Revenge, for all the mental backlash Dominion and I received, because of what he's done to Kendra. Now was the perfect time to pursue my plan before Leo, destroyed Kendra, as well as everything and everybody around her.

CHAPTER XVIII

All day long, I've been driving around, executing my plan. I had gone and bought myself some gloves, a ski mask, black clothing, and most importantly, a pistol. For the pistol, I had to pull up on Chris' cousin, Bubba. Bubba, who is originally from around Mayfair apartments, hangs out not too far up the street from my apartment building. I remembered, years ago when Chris made it clear that if I was ever faced with a situation that I couldn't handle and he was unavailable to assist me, that I could just pull-up on Bubba. Chris said, if Bubba couldn't handle it himself, he would for sure point me in the right direction. Chris, introduced us once before, and we greeted each other at Chris' funeral, but we never really sat down and held a real conversation. We would honk our horn and wave at each other in passing, but that was about it. So, when I pulled up on Bubba, he knew immediately that I needed a favor. After I told Bubba what I needed, with no questions asked, he handed me a .357 Magnum.

"From the looks of things, you tryna get your man." Bubba explained. "This right here leaves no shell casings behind, and will leave a hole in your opp head the size of a G-Shock watch."

From the moment that I saw that piece of chrome, my palms were sweating.

I'd talked to Kendra earlier this morning when she first opened the salon, but haven't heard anything from her since. I've been constantly ringing her phone to pinpoint her whereabouts for the past half hour and still, NOTHING! Her phone will ring a few times before going to the voicemail. I've left her a voice message and left multiple text messages, but still no reply.

PHONE RINGING

"Totally Amazing Barber and Beauty Salon, Tanya speaking." The voice on the other side of the phone said.

"Hey Tanya, this Derrick. You saw Kendra?" I calmly asked.

"Not for about an hour or so. She said she had to go run some errands and stop past her house to check something out. She been here all day before that." Tanya explained, while popping her chewing gum on the other side of the line.

"Damn. She not answering her phone or my messages. If she reach out to you, tell her to hit my phone ASAP, okay?"

"Okay, you know I got you, Derrick." Tanya flirted, with a giggle.

"Yeah, aight," I flirted back. "Thanks, Tanya."

"Anytime, boo." Tanya whispered, before hanging up.

PHONE RINGING

"Hello!" Leo answered, sounding as if he were out of breath.

"Leo, wassup slim, you saw Kendra today?" I aggressively asked.

Leo, knew I wasn't too fond of him, and I surely struggled with trying to hide my differences towards him.

"Kendra? No-no, bro I haven't." Leo replied nervously, sounding fatigued. "I've been looking for her too. She was supposed to have stopped past the house before I got here, but it doesn't look like she ever showed up. I'ma sit here and wait for about another hour or so, before I head out to go pick up Dominion. Hopefully she calls one of us back by then."

Leo was always acting nervous anytime he was around me or on the phone with me so, that was no surprise. One thing he wasn't good at, was disguising his fear of my presence. That alone let me know that he was full of shit.

"Yeah, hopefully." I replied.

"Well, if she calls me or pops up before I leave out, I'll give you a call, bro." Leo assured.

"Yeah, let me know 'cause I need to rap to her ASAP."

"Okay, gotcha." Leo replied, before hanging up the line.

"What the fuck is up with Leo?" I mumbled to myself out of curiosity.

Whatever it was, I wasn't planning to find out. I was too focused executing my plan of attack. Matter of fact, right now is the perfect time to execute my plan and honestly, I might never get a perfect opportunity like this one again. Dominion, is at the babysitters' house, and Kendra, is possibly laid up somewhere with Eric. So, by the time she gets home, I would be long gone in the wind.

CHAPTER XIX

I pulled up directly across the street from Kendra's house on 16th and Buchanan Street at exactly 8:28 pm and surveyed the premises. I then circled around the block to see if I saw either the police, Leo or Kendra's car, and saw neither. I did notice a light shining through their garage window. Kendra and Leo's garage was located behind their house on a backstreet called Piney Branch Drive and, due to the way it's designed, I couldn't tell whether or not a vehicle was inside of the garage simply from driving past but I could see that a light was turned on, through the small windows. After my brief survey, I decided to park on the sixteen-hundred block of Crittenden Street, on the side of Nineteenth Street Baptist Church.

To this day, I still wonder why it was called 'Nineteenth Street Baptist Church' when it was located on 16th Street. Something I'll investigate later. After I cut off the engine, I retrieved the .357 revolver from the glove compartment and tucked it inside of my waistline. I then placed my car keys in my pocket before getting out of the car and pacing over to the fifteen-hundred block of Crittenden Street, making a right turn onto Piney Branch Drive. I then cut through a neighboring yard before I ended up in Kendra's backyard. The rear entrance was the smarter choice due to the constant traffic on 16th Street. Tonight, it was dark outside and calm for the most part.

I took a peek inside of the small windows on the garage and saw Leo's car inside, but not Kendra's. 'Perfect!' I thought to myself. I then crept through the backyard up to the back door. I first pulled the ski mask down over my face before I fitted the key into the lock, clicked it open and entered their home. As soon as I walked into the house, I heard rattling sounds and a loud thump coming from towards the kitchen area. I immediately removed the pistol from my waistline and clutched it in the palm of my hand with my pointer finger resting on the trigger. As I quietly closed the door, I reminded myself to immediately destroy the lock on the backdoor to make it look like a forced entry after I kill Leo. As I crept through the house towards the kitchen area, the noises became louder. A lot of movement and heavy breathing is what it sounded like.

"SHIT! FUCK! WHY!" Leo's voice yelled out as I leaned my back onto the wall outside of the kitchen area. I can admit, I was scared. I had never in my lifetime done anything even close to what I had planned. But I'm here now! I took a deep breath before I spun around the wall in a one hundred eighty-degree angle, appearing inside of the kitchen entrance, pistol hoisted high, pointing in the direction of where Leo was standing. Leo had his back turned toward me as he stood in the middle of the kitchen floor, slightly leaned over and staring down at something I assumed was on the floor. I couldn't view what he was staring at because of the kitchen counter which blocked my view.

"Hands up, mothafucka!" I spat, disguising my voice with a Jamaican accent.

Leo's body immediately tensed up in fear as he slowly turned around to face me, his eyes as big as golf balls.

"Hands on the counter, mothafucka!" I instructed Leo.

He quickly did as I ordered, and placed his hands onto the counter top, as I slowly paced toward him, creeping around the kitchen counter to see what had caught his stare. To see....

To see what I was not expecting to see. A BODY!

Mummy wrapped in plastic in what looked like a blanket underneath of the plastic. The body was stretched out on the kitchen floor, leaving me in shock. I couldn't believe what I was seeing. I then looked up into Leo's nervous face, who also seemed to be stuck in shock, as he just stared at me. I then looked back down to analyze the body, and noticed the feet sticking from out of the bottom.

"The ankle bracelet!" It was…

Kendra's! Kendra's ankle bracelet! Kendra's foot! Kendra's body! Unable to fully breathe, I stared at Leo's face before forcing out,

"Kendra!"

"Derrick?" Leo replied out of confusion and fear. "Brother, you have to hear me out! Kendra made me do it, brother! She was cheating on me, bro!" Leo frantically explained, as I stood over top of Kendra's body, staring angrily at Leo with the pistol pointed toward his chest. I then removed the ski mask and dropped it onto the floor. BLOCKA! BLOCKA! The first two shots spun Leo's body around in a ninety-degree angle, as he stumbled and fell into wall located about five feet behind him. Leo sat on the floor up against the wall, clutching his chest as he coughed up clots of blood. I then walked over towards him within point blank range and pointed the pistol in his face before I squeezed. BLOCKA! BLOCKA! BLOCKA! CLICK! CLICK! CLICK! CLICK! CLICK! CLICK! CLICK! Three bullets in his face, with the intention of more. Numb and traumatized was how I felt. I was far from my normal self. I knew that after tonight I would never be the same Derrick Jones. The little shy kid was long gone and was reborn into a humble man with a vengeance. My palms went from sweaty to dry in a matter of seconds, as if I were a contracted killer. As I stood staring over Leo's lifeless body for several minutes, the pistol dropped out of my hand. I then turned towards Kendra's body, walked over to her and sat down beside her. I then began to unwrap Kendra's body from out of the materials before cradling her lifeless body in my arms. I just held her, and cried.

CHAPTER XX

HEY NEPHEW. HOW'S IT GOING? I PRAY THAT ALLAH BLESS YOU WITH A SECOND CHANCE IN LIFE. YOU'RE A GOOD MAN AND DONE WHAT ANY "REAL MAN" IN YOUR POSITION WOULD'VE DONE. PROTECT YOUR FAMILY! WHATEVER YOU NEED ME TO DO JUST LET ME KNOW. THEY GAVE ME 6 MONTHS HALFWAY HOUSE. I BEEN IN HERE FOR ABOUT A MONTH NOW. MY GOOD MAN LOU HAS BEEN KEEPING ME BLESSED UP. HE'S A REAL GOOD MAN LIKE YOURSELF WITH A HISTORICAL BLOODLINE. I'M VERY FAMILIAR WITH HIS COUSINS AND FAMILY. I WASN'T TOO FOND OF THEM BUT IT WILL ALL PLAY ITSELF OUT IN DUE TIME NEPHEW. ALWAYS REMEMBER, WHEN IT COMES TO PROTECTING THE HONOR OF YOUR FAMILY, THERE ARE NO LIMITS! BE A CHAMELEON AND USE YOUR RESOURCES.

I WILL KEEP YOU UPDATED AND MAKE SURE YOU WRITE ME BACK NEPHEW.   AND CHECK YOUR ACCOUNT, I SENT YOU SOMETHING. LOVE YOU BIG BOY!

SINCERELY,
    UNCLE MIKE

It's been four years since I lost Kendra, and honestly, I can still feel the same fire in my heart every time that I think of her. My attitude towards life has gotten worse, and I've become somewhat of a villain in a lot of ways. I stabbed three dudes since I been in prison. Two, when I was locked up in DC jail, fighting my case, and only one other since I've been housed in the FBOP. I've been locked up in *USP Canaan*, in Waymart, Pennsylvania, for about two years now, awaiting direct appeal. We have several issues that we're arguing to get my conviction overturned, but the main issue we're banking on is "IN THE HEAT OF PASSION". That's one argument that my trial lawyer never argued during our trial, which is part of my ineffective assistance of counsel claim. I sat in DC jail and fought this case for two years, just to lose trial to first degree murder, second degree murder, attempted robbery and several other minor charges. I was sentenced to seven hundred-twenty months, in prison. Now, I'm trying to figure out where in the hell I was supposed to start doing all this time at. What is considered the beginning? That is one thing I probably would never know, but I damn sure do know how to start the ending of it, and that's in the law library.

In the past four years while fighting this murder case, I've learned a lot about Leo. More than I think Kendra would've ever known about him in a lifetime. My appeal and trial attorneys made it very clear to me that Leo, came from a really troubled and disturbing past, which caused tremendous mental health abuse. I mean, where do I start? First, Leo, witnessed his mom being physically abused by his dad on a daily basis, before his mom shot his father, and left him paralyzed before fatally shooting herself in the head after thinking that she had killed him. Leo, was instructed by his dad to dial 9-1-1, as he watched his dad lay on the bed and choke on his own blood while his mom laid stretched out on the floor with a bullet in her head. Leo, was only twelve years young at this time. I was also informed that exactly one year later, Leo's father had allegedly fell out of his wheelchair, down a flight of stairs in their home, and broke his neck. Leo, again, was the one who had dialed 9-1-1 after finding his dad dead. Afterwards, he was placed into a foster home and was never adopted.

In 2007, Leo, was investigated for the disappearance of his ex-wife and mother of his child. They had went of a vacation trip to Aruba, where she mysteriously disappeared. Her body was never discovered, and that case remains an unsolved mystery. I was told that her family had argued to the media, and District Attorneys, that Leo, was highly abusive to his wife and that they adamantly believed that Leo was behind her disappearance. But there was no proof to support their claims, and those claims were considered accusations and speculation.

After hearing and learning all of what I now know about Leo's past, on top of him murdering Kendra, I actually felt proud of myself. I felt justified. And that justification made the fact that I lost trial a whole lot easier to fathom.

"Slim, I think he got some more mail for you, champ." My celly Smokey Black said, as he stood by the door looking out of the window into the day room, during the mid-day 4 pm count.

The C/O was walking around the housing unit, sliding our mail under our room doors. My celly, Smokey Black, whose real name is Obi Aku, was an African dude who was claiming Mayfair Apartments, as his stomping grounds. At least that's what he was saying. The only thing that made me slightly believe his claim was that he was always talking about the dude named Lou. That was the same guy that my Uncle Mike mentioned. I reckon slim was getting some real cash around there. I explained to Smokey Black how I once lived around Mayfair, as a kid, but never hung around there after we moved on Gault Place. Though we were so close in distance, I never once remembered seeing Smokey Black. To me, Smokey Black, was a well-rounded, solid dude. He was older than me, about 32 years old, so I considered him to be my OG. Smokey Black had been in prison for about two or three years now, but has only been my celly for roughly two weeks. He initially came to prison before his current case, for a triple homicide in which he got acquitted, then came back a few months later for another murder indictment. He lost trial to first degree murder, and was sentenced to nine hundred months in prison. Smokey Black, wasn't a bad guy, and I felt that he deserved to be a free man. And from learning the little details about his case that he felt comfortable sharing, his freedom seemed inevitable.

"Here you go, fool. You got big mail." Smokey Black joked, as he handed me my mail while I was sitting up on the bottom bunk, just finishing reading my uncle Mike's letter.

"Thanks, champ." I replied, as I looked through the two pieces of mail I had just received. One piece read, *DC COURT OF APPEALS*, and the other read, SARAH MANGELLI. Sarah!? Wow! I was eager to know how she had been doing, so I decided to open her letter first...

It's been 4 years now and I've decided that now is the perfect time to reach out to you for closure. I've been wanting to write you for years, but couldn't figure out where to start. I just want to let you know that I am sorry for everything that has happened and wish it all could've been different. I've realized, I lost a lot but you have lost more. I can admit that I was bitter and upset for the first couple of years, but after a few counseling sessions, I've overcame what I cannot control. I'm now older and 7 months pregnant, expecting my first child. It's supposed to be a boy. I would be honored if you named him. Well, I pray on your appeals success, and hope you are released soon. May God bless you and stay strong. I will be expecting a letter back soon.

Sincerely,

Sarah

Wow! It's really been that long, huh? Young Sarah is pregnant, and understanding. I'ma make it my business to write her back tonight. I've been wondering about her well-being. I wonder if she can help me find my nephew Dominion. I would love to hear from him, or just see a photo of him.

After placing Sarah's letter back into the envelope that it had come in, I quickly opened the letter from the *DC Court of Appeals*, and just like that, my heart skipped a beat. I couldn't believe what I was reading.

> "You good?" Smokey Black asked me, as he analyzed my facial expression. I then handed him the letter without saying a word. I was at a loss for words.

> "Oh yeah!" Smokey Black yelled out of excitement, before he shook my hand and embraced me, celebrating my success.

The *DC Court of Appeals* gave me some play and overturned my conviction. Soon, I will be on my way back to court for a hearing and possibly a retrial. I was feeling blessed and highly excited. Smokey Black and I celebrated and talked about my plans of when I finally do hit the streets. He offered me a lot of good advice, and I was taking heed. The sun was finally shining in my direction, like it was supposed to. At least until....

"Aye, bruh, you ain't get to meet the new homie yet, did you?" Smokey Black, asked me while he was washing his hands in the sink.

"Nah, where he at?" I replied.

"He over there in the cell with Black Joe. He supposed to be from around your side of town too, playboy." Smokey Black said, as he dried his hands before walking back over to the door to look into the dayroom. "Y'all might know each other. Slim say he been locked up for 'bout five years now."

"Oh yeah?" I questioned out of curiosity. "What he say his name was?"

"Man, I forgot what he said."

"Did you get to see his laundry bag?"

"You know what, I sure did." Smokey Black replied excitedly, with a chuckle. "That joint said 'R. Edwards', if I ain't mistaken."

"Edwards!?" I exclaimed, before standing up from off the bed, and walking over towards the doorway to look out of the window into the empty dayroom.

Smokey Black, simultaneously moved past me toward the lockers in the back of the room, giving me my personal space to survey the unit.

"What, you know slim?" Smokey Black asked.

"How he look?" I questioned.

"He an ol' ugly looking ass nigga. Creep in the face looking ass nigga." Smokey Black joked, as he hopped up on the top bunk bed before kicking off his shoes.

"That nigga name Flip!?" I asked Smokey Black wide-eyedly, which triggered him to snap and point his finger in my direction as if I had solved a murder mystery.

"Bingo! That's exactly what that nigga said his name was…. Flip!"

To Be Continued….

Made in the USA
Monee, IL
01 April 2023

31055045R00073